7

To Charlie & Tom —

Charlie on a belated
birthday present, Thank you
thank you for your expert
expert and help in making
this happen!

Love Always,

[signature]

The Snowflake Collector

The Snowflake Collector

by Sebastian Michael

Illustrated by Diego Cassia

optimistbooks.com

First Edition

The Snowflake Collector was first published online as part of *EDEN by FREI – a concept narrative in the here & now about the where, the wherefore and forever* at EDENbyFREI.net

ISBN 978-1-68418-180-3

Optimist Books by Optimist Creations

optimistcreations.com

1: Barely the End of October

Up at the end of the valley, the far end, before it yields to the glacier which reaches down from the mountain pass, slowly receding now with growing temperatures, lives an old man who looks at the world still with wonder.

He is not as old as he seems at first glance, and much older than his years all the same, for he knows. He knows, deep inside, what holds the universe together and what tears it apart and what being these molecules, what being that energy means. He knows it but he can't express it, and so he won't. He won't talk about it, he won't, in fact, talk about anything much, he appreciates silence.

When he was young he used to meet up with friends for a drink and a chinwag, and then it began to dawn on him that much of what he was being told, and even more of what he heard himself speak, was an array of variations on themes: things he'd heard said and had spoken before, in this way, or that, or another. Self-perpetuating reiterations of what everybody already knew and keenly agreed on, or hotly disputed, as was their whim.

And so he let go, he let go of his friends whom he loved but could no longer bring himself to like, and let go of the circuitous conversations that did nothing but remind everybody that they were still who they thought they needed to want to be. He was tired. And being tired he got old, older than his years, older than his looks, older than the oak tree in the oldest garden. And he moved, once or twice first, then twice or thrice more, and each move took him further away from those whom he had been, had made himself feel, acquainted with. First to the country, then to the coast, then the foreign lands, then the mountains, then the valley and then the end of the valley, in the mountains again: the remotest place he could find.

It was not that he was happy here, it was just that he was content. Content not to need to desire happiness any more. And here he sat and walked. Sat by the house he'd bought for very little, and walked over the fields and the meadows and up to the vantage points from which he could see the peaks and the woods and the villages, in the very great distance. He liked that distance: distance was space, distance was calm, distance was perspective. Unencumberedness. Distance was good.

Winter came to the valley and it was barely the end of October, and going for walks now was harder because everything was covered in snow. And this being the far end of the remotest valley he could find, nobody came to clear the snow or pave the paths or even the lane that led up to his hut. So he was stuck, in a way, and he liked being stuck, it meant, in a way, being safe. Safe from visitors, safe from the desire to go out, safe from choices. The persistent demand of decisions, abjured. Simplicity. He'd craved that. And now, he had it.

What he was able to do still was sit on the bench in front of his hut and watch the world go by. Except the world didn't go by here, it stood pretty much still. Or so it would seem. And he knew, of course, that this wasn't true, that nothing stood still, that everything was in motion, always. He found it comforting. Disconcerting too, but comforting; and he had said so. He'd said so and had been quoted as saying so too.

With each day that passed, winter became more present and more unreal: the snowflakes tumbling from the skies like clumsy, half-frozen bumble bees out of a freezer up in the cloud. There was something in him still that reminded him of the kindness of people, and he let one or two of these snowflakes alight on his hand, and they melted and ceased to exist. How sad, he thought to himself, how just and, yes, how poetic. And he recalled once upon a time being a poet, and that's when he decided to capture and keep them. Not all of them, obviously, only some. And to collect them. To preserve them. He knew this was futile and went against nature, but therein exactly lay the exquisite sensation of thrill and deep satisfaction. To do something that was futile and that went against nature, but that would be indescribably beautiful. That was more than existing, that went beyond breathing and eating and sleeping and defecating and shaking in anger and dreaming and imagining and sitting and thinking: that was living. That was imbuing the accidental presence of clusters of mass-manifest energy in this constellation with something that surpassed everything, something divine, something purposeful and profound, something quintessentially and incomparably human: meaning.

2: His Task Would Be Immense

At first he didn't know how to collect snowflakes; he did not even know whether it was possible to do so at all. All he knew was that if he were able to preserve and collect snowflakes, then he would have something meaningful to do for the rest of his days, because there would never come a day when he would chance upon a snowflake that would be identical to any he already had in his collection, and so his collection would never be complete.

This, he also already knew, would be both infuriating and reassuring. There would be times when he would feel like throwing out all the carefully crafted wooden cases, into which would slide all the cautiously cut plates of glass, upon which would rest – for the relative eternity of any civilisation in existence being conscious of them, let alone able to appreciate them – the snowflakes in their time-frozen state, and burning the lot in a bonfire. But he would not do so, he was certain, for deep down he knew how precious his collection would become, and how singular, how unique.

The wood for the carefully crafted cases would come from the firs on his land by the stream. Since he heated his hut in the cold months with wood from his land by the stream, he planted two young firs to replace each mature one he cut down, and this way, he thought, the balance in the valley (and therefore in the universe) would stay intact, even tilt a little in favour of trees, with his presence.

He knew well how to craft wooden cases, even intricate ones as these would undoubtedly have to be, because they would need to have slits in them at regular intervals, just so spaced and so fashioned that a small plate of glass, in size about one inch by three, would slide easily in and out of the case, but stay firmly in place once stowed. The cases would have to be sturdy and each have a handle, so they in turn could glide effortlessly – apart from their weight, which would be considerable – in and out of a larger box, and this larger box would need to be stackable, because he knew that over time he would collect snowflakes enough to fill many of them. He would have to, he realised, build a shed. And he would build that shed from the same fir trees that stood on his land by the stream.

It was clear to him now that his task would be immense. Because not only would he have to carefully craft wooden cases, and for these wooden cases strong wooden boxes, and for these boxes a formidable shed, he would have to cut glass into regular plates, one inch by three, on which he would capture the snowflakes. And he would have to catalogue them. He felt unsure about how to catalogue snowflakes, since he had no experience or expertise in this, but as with most things that he had ever attempted in his life before, he also thought that he would find a way. What didn't appeal to him was the thought of giving his snowflakes numbers. Numbers, he felt, when they are not being used for elegant thinking, are not poetic, certainly not poetic enough to record snowflakes. No, he was sure, from the very first moment, even before he had gone out to collect his first snowflake, that he would have to name them. And since – as everyone knows and he knew – each snowflake would be different, he would just have to find a specific name for each one.

As he sat down, that evening, outside his hut, having so made his decision to collect the snowflakes – not all of them, only some – and contemplated the great task ahead of him, and experienced the tremendous delight in not knowing which snowflakes he would catch and collect, and which snowflakes would elude him, and therefore what names he would have to find for those snowflakes he would keep, he felt a deep glow of happiness fill his heart. This is who I shall become, he thought to himself: The Snowflake Collector.

3: 'I Need to Know How to Collect Snowflakes'

While he knew well how to craft wooden cases, and for these wooden cases build sturdy boxes and for the sturdy boxes – many as there would be – construct a formidable shed, and had the tools in his hut and the fir trees on his land by the stream to make all these things, and while he also possessed a diamond glass cutter and knew where to find good solid flat glass to cut into precisely dimensioned plates of three inches by one, over time in very large numbers, The Snowflake Collector did not know how to collect snowflakes.

He had never before given any thought to the possibility that he might one day decide to collect snowflakes and thus become The Snowflake Collector, but now that he had determined to do so – as certain and as irrevocable as if it had been set in stone, and yet, of course, from a wider, much longer perspective, as transient too – he felt compelled to research the matter, in detail.

It would have appealed to his great sense of distance, which he had so sought out and which he so cherished, to undertake a long journey and walk down into the valley and from there take the yellow bus to the very small town and from there take a little red train to the nearest small city and from there a bigger and faster and greener or whiter train to the bigger (though still fairly small) city and there go to the large stately library kept by the university and ask a bespectacled and certainly not hostile but perhaps slightly weary librarian for a book on Snowflake Collecting, but he knew that such an excursion, which entailed the expense of time and resources, was an unnecessary and therefore wasteful exertion, and while he did not believe that time could really be expended any more than it could be kept in a jar, he nevertheless found any temptation that might have drawn him from his valley and into the city, overpowered, readily, easily, by the comfort and safety of his mountains.

So, instead, he walked down to the inn, an hour or so from his hut, in the outpost hamlet some few miles from the village, and there he was greeted with a smile by Yolanda, the waitress from the Ukraine. Yolanda had come from the Ukraine to find work here as a waitress, and she liked the landlord, because the landlord was not interested in her, he mostly spent his time with his mostly young friends. Like everyone else, Yolanda knew The Snowflake Collector, although she, like everyone else, did not know yet that that's who he was. She greeted him with her smile that she never needed to force and started pulling a dark ale for him because in all the years she had known (or thought that she'd known) him (for nobody really knew him at all), he had never wanted anything other than a dark ale from the tap.

'Is Yanosh around?' he asked her, having thanked her, as she brought the heavy beaker to him at the table in the corner with a small view out of the square window onto some very brown cows.

'He is, I can call him for you if you like?'

'When he's not busy.'

The Snowflake Collector knew that Yanosh would not be busy now, because Yanosh was Yolanda's son of about fifteen, and he didn't like his peers down in the village too much, so he mainly kept himself to himself in his room, playing games on the computer or writing songs which he never played to anyone, or fantasising about travelling back in time to the past or forward into the future, or being naked with an actress he had recently started to fancy.

Yanosh came down directly when his mother asked him if he would, because he liked The Snowflake Collector, and although he didn't know yet that that's who he was either, he, unlike almost anyone else in the world, sensed that he did know him a bit. They both knew each other, a bit. And they liked each other for knowing each other a bit, but not more, and for mainly leaving each other alone but when necessary being able to spend time in each other's company without ever having to say or do anything.

Sometimes, when he felt particularly bored or lonely or uncertain why he was even here, or just wanted to be out of his room, but not anywhere where there were people, but also not anywhere where there were none, Yanosh would stomp up that same path that The Snowflake Collector had just come down now, and simply sit outside his hut, in the sun, or if there was no sun, then in the rain. It didn't matter to Yanosh whether there was sunshine or rain, or no rain but clouds: he liked sitting outside The Snowflake Collector's hut, because here he could sit in absolute peace with no demands being made on him and simply watch the world go by, which it didn't, up here, because up here, the world stood pretty much still; but Yanosh, much as The Snowflake Collector, knew of course that nothing stood still, that everything was in motion, always, and while Yanosh did not find this either disconcerting or comforting – he had little need, in his life, yet, for disconcertion or comfort – he nevertheless found it soothing. And sometimes The Snowflake Collector would already be sitting there too and they would nod at each other and perhaps mutter 'hello', though with hardly any tone to their voice at all, and then sit there; and sometimes The Snowflake Collector would not be around but would find him there and join him, and they would similarly nod at each other or, not expending any unnecessary breath on words, perhaps mutter 'hello', perhaps not even that, but sit there in great silence, which they both so greatly appreciated, Yanosh quite as much as The Snowflake Collector.

Over the years that Yanosh had come to sit with The Snowflake Collector, there would have been the occasional short conversation, sometimes perhaps inside the hut, over a glass of *Chrüterschnapps* or with a slice of *Bündnerfleisch,* and so The Snowflake Collector knew that if he ever found himself in need of any information at all, the person to ask was Yanosh, because Yanosh spent most of his waking hours – when he wasn't sitting with him here in front of his hut or in his very small kitchen – on his smartphone or his computer, and he therefore had access, any time night or day, to all the knowledge in the world, if perhaps not all of its wisdom.

Yanosh sat down and they nodded at each other their familiar nod that did not demand any words, and The Snowflake Collector said, to the querying glance of the youth, who in spite of his pain never once betrayed any sorrow:

'I need to know how to collect snowflakes.'

4: And He Had Many Memories

The Snowflake Collector was a lone man, but he was not lonely. He had in Yanosh a friend and in Yolanda a friendly face, and he had many memories, some solidifying like ice that is formed by the weight of the snow in the glacier, and others fading like snowflakes alighting atop a meadow too early in the year, or too late, and melting away with the first rays of the sun, much as the first snow in October had already melted and was no more now, and no less, than a harbinger, that had been and gone, of what was to come.

And also of what was to go: it would come and cover the earth and the path and the mind for much longer soon, throughout the winter and into spring, but go it eventually would. But during those cold months this year for the first time, and in all coming years left him for as many times as were in the gift of his existence, he would now collect snowflakes. The cows in the meadow he could see from the very small window in the very thick wall of the inn, which had already been covered once, briefly, with snow, looked forlorn now, a little, but also quite safe, because they were already near their barn and soon they would disappear in there for the winter.

He considered, while Yanosh went online with his smartphone to look up 'how to collect snowflakes' on the connected brain of the world, how each snowflake was perhaps like a memory, and that there would be, in a lifetime, as many memories as there were snowflakes in a season, though what these memories were – much as what these snowflakes would look like – depended a great deal on the era, the region, the weather, of course, and the altitude, and the many, maybe innumerable, larger and smaller contributing factors, both literal and metaphorical, such as the overall climate and topography, the circumstances and constellations, the chemicals and the particles (be they natural or man-made) in the air.

If every memory is a bit like a snowflake and every snowflake therefore a bit like a memory, then I shall collect these snowflakes like memories, and like memories they will be an artifice, in my collection, much as pictures in an album are a curated but also distorted reflection of memories, and they will be an artifice because in nature snowflakes will either solidify into ice and form layer upon layer of no longer distinguishable single delicate structures but the body of matter that is the glacier, or they will melt away with the sun, sometimes maybe having served a purpose – such as providing a surface for skiers to glide down the mountainside on – but more often not.

'It's really easy,' Yanosh said after just a few minutes of such contemplative silence, during which, The Snowflake Collector noted with some delight, it had started gently snowing again outside already, 'you just need some superglue or hairspray or something to fix them onto your glass plates with; you freeze down the glass plate first so the flake doesn't melt, then you dab or spray on the fixing agent and you put your snowflake on it, or let one settle: what you get in effect is an imprint of the snowflake, then you cover that with another glass plate to protect it, and you're done.'

The Snowflake Collector breathed a silent sigh of relief. He had not expected snowflake collecting to be difficult, but he knew, from many long years of experience – as he felt he'd experienced them, though they weren't that many, and they had not been any longer than any other years, except for the leap years that fell in between the ordinary ones, which had been just one day longer – that sometimes the simplest thing can turn out to be fiendishly complicated, and conversely sometimes the most daunting and difficult task can simply ebb away and turn out to be nothing more than a thing that just needed to be done. So finding, upon the reliable research carried out by Yanosh on his behalf there and then, that snowflake collecting was 'really easy' came, to The Snowflake Collector, as a relief, and as confirmation – though no such confirmation was needed – that he was on the right track, that he had found his calling, that the universe, at least this universe that he believed himself to be part of at this moment, was welcoming him into – perhaps even bestowing upon him – this role; and since he had already determined, as irrevocably as could reasonably (or even quite unreasonably) be maintained, to be The Snowflake Collector, this meant that he and the universe were not now at odds but in tune with each other. And for that thought alone, The Snowflake Collector felt immeasurably relieved but also grateful and calm; almost happy, although he did not, by and large, entertain any notion of, or great desire for, 'happiness', finding it to be so very unreliable and unsound a concept, but certainly, and this was the realisation that cheered him so greatly, at one with the universe. Had he not longed so long just for that, to be at one with the universe.

5: He Had Abandoned the Notion of 'Hurry'

With daylight hours gradually usurped by darkness now, and cooler, longer nights now spreading their still presence over the valley, The Snowflake Collector set about his endeavour.

After the early snowfall towards the end of October, which had soon ceased and given way to one more spell of golden autumn with spice in the air, winter had now been sending more heralds, tentatively, at first, but unmistakably nonetheless, and welcome. While he knew now how to collect snowflakes and knew what things he needed to obtain, and what things to make, before he could do so, The Snowflake Collector was in no hurry. It had been many years since he had last allowed the world to impose on him any 'hurry', and it had revealed itself to him so futile then, so unnecessary and unnecessarily restless, that he had abandoned the notion of 'hurry' altogether, never to seek it out again, or permit it to return.

It would suffice completely, he knew, to collect one, maybe two snowflakes to begin with. Better, he thought to himself, do this and do this well than to rush into constructing a shed – indispensable as it would undoubtedly be – or building the sturdy boxes for the delicately crafted cases. No, he would build a case, yes, from wood he had already stored under the roof by the side of his hut, and he would cut some plates from glass he knew where to buy, and he would use some of the superglue that had been languishing in his tool box for years, but never been opened, and he would collect one or two, or maybe three snowflakes and see how that felt, how at home they would be in the case he would build.

So when Yanosh next wandered up the narrow path towards the end of the valley to sit outside The Snowflake Collector's hut and maybe nod 'hello' at him, maybe not, he found him there in the late autumn sunshine sawing pieces of wood. He was not a master carpenter, The Snowflake Collector, but he had for many years now been living on his own in his hut, and soon after moving here he had purchased, for very little money, a small plot of land further down the valley, right by the stream, where there were already some firs, and where he now planted, for every old one he cut down, two young trees; and so he had, over time, gained enough experience making things out of wood to do so confidently, and well. Yanosh nodded what may have been a 'hello' to The Snowflake Collector, and The Snowflake Collector understood and nodded back what to most people might have been barely perceptible, but to Yanosh, with similar certainty, signalled 'hello'.

It would often be the case now that Yanosh would find The Snowflake Collector thus or otherwise engaged in preparing his snowflake collection. He never explained what he was doing, and Yanosh never asked, as to both it was obvious, but Yanosh enjoyed watching The Snowflake Collector at work, because there was a calm determination and purpose to his labour, and The Snowflake Collector was at ease in these tasks, for the very same reason. Sometimes Yanosh would hold up a long plank of wood or pass a tool or pick up a piece of glass that had fallen to the ground, but mostly he would just sit there and watch as The Snowflake Collector went about his new business.

Having never collected snowflakes before, or anything else for that matter, it did not surprise The Snowflake Collector, and nor did it surprise Yanosh, that everything did not go smoothly.

The first case he built, although beautiful and smooth, with clean but not sharp edges and a convenient handle at the narrow top, turned out to be useless as it was simply too large. It had looked, in The Snowflake Collector's imagination, and in his rudimentary drawings which were not quite to scale, exactly right, but it came out not so. Once he had filled it with glass plates, each three inches long and one inch wide, it was too heavy for him to lift easily off his work bench, and so he started over again.

He also realised only now that he would not, after all, need to build sturdy boxes for these cases. He would simply have to build the cases themselves sturdy enough, and for the cases he would have to construct a formidable shed in which he would need to fit strong shelves evenly spaced, but there was no need, in reality, for another, intermediate layer of housing for his snowflakes, just as long as the cases were sound.

It was not until the second week of December that The Snowflake Collector was ready to collect his first snowflake. By then he had made and destroyed a first case for snowflakes that had turned out to be unwieldy and large, and he had made and dismantled a second case, which had been the right size and shape, but in which the glass plates that were to hold the snowflakes did not sit snugly enough, but rattled when he closed the lid and lifted the case off the bench, and this, The Snowflake Collector was certain, would not do. Having dismantled the case, he then saw that there was no easy way to fix the inadequacy, say by adjusting the slot width for the glass plates which had too much give, and so he discarded this second case too and made a third, better one. This, he found, when he slid all the glass plates he had by now cut from large sheets of plain glass – cutting himself several times in the process and once very painfully so – to be, if not perfect, then sufficiently solid and sturdy and strong.

By now there had been snowfall on several more occasions. But The Snowflake Collector was glad that circumstances had conspired, and maybe he and his subconscious mind had conspired with them, to make him wait until now, until very nearly the beginning of winter, before he commenced his immense undertaking. He was not a stickler for rules, and it would have disquieted, even appalled, him to know himself one who awaited the 'official' date for the start of the season, or anything else, but if there was one thing The Snowflake Collector believed to be true then it was that to every thing there *is* a season, and while he had not given it any elaborate or conscious thought, he felt instinctively that the time for collecting snowflakes had not come, until now.

Now, towards the end of the second week of December, with the feast of St Nicholas already gone and the days in the valley short now and sombre when the sun wasn't shining, and crisp and cold and still very short when it was, The Snowflake Collector woke up one morning from a night of fitful sleep with no dream that he could recall, and as he opened his eyes and glanced from his narrow hard bed to the small cross-hatched window, which in all the years he had lived here had never been curtained, he saw that there was snow on the sill and there were big heavy snowflakes tumbling again from the sky, as there had been on that day when he had resolved to become The Snowflake Collector, which now seemed eternities in the past, but which was only in fact some six weeks ago, at barely the end of October.

His heart leapt at the sight, because he knew that this was the day, that the hour had come, that the convergence of all things leading up to now had finally made this Now possible, and real. With calm, serene joy, he rose from his bed, lit the fire in the stove, performed his rudimentary and no more than essential ablutions, dressed warmly and went to the kitchen where, in a small freezer compartment of his small refrigerator he had chilled a small stack of glass plates, much as Yanosh had instructed him to.

With three of them he went outside, picking up from the kitchen drawer the small tube of superglue he had placed there in preparation, and in front of his hut he put everything down on his bench. There he carefully dabbed a drop of glue on a frozen glass plate and, holding the plate in his hand, raised his eyes to the sky.

6: A Snowflake Not Unlike Him

Some of the snowflakes came down in clusters, others in twirling jumbles, and others still in flighty twists, but he knew he needed a steady snowflake that was on its own, a lone snowflake, disentangled, unburdened, unencumbered, free: a snowflake not unlike him, a snowflake that had been gently descending along its unspectacular way through the world and was now ready to leave its most particular, most individual mark.

Such a snowflake soon caught his eye, as it approached, a little slower than some of the clumpier ones around it and a little faster than some of the ones that didn't quite seem formed yet, and he held out his bare hand with the glass plate on it, and as if a little curious, as if attracted, as if called by this strip of translucence in its path, it settled, and lo: it stayed. Like a bed made for it, like a throne on which now to sit, like a home that was primed now and ready for it there to live, the snowflake accepted this destination and delivered its presence onto the plate, its intricate shape, its form, its identity kissed into the fast drying liquid.

The Snowflake Collector looked at his treasure in sheer wonder. My dear good friend, I can't presume to know you, but may I name you Ferdinand. The snowflake did not object to being so named and The Snowflake Collector solemnly took him inside, looked at him closely, as closely as he could with his bare eyes, under the light, and he dabbed one more drop of superglue over him to fix him and then lay another glass plate on top of Ferdinand, to protect him. Also, he realised, to encase him: his bed, his throne, was also his tomb.

A deep pain and anguish drove through The Snowflake Collector's heart at this moment: am I committing a crime, am I stealing Ferdinand's soul? Should he not have been allowed to ease himself onto the ground or the bench or the table, among his companions, and then melt away with the sun, seep into the ground, dissolve into his watery molecules and find his way back into the rhythm of the universe? Is my keeping him captive here now for as long as these glass plates will last not depriving his spirit from turning into something else, something different, but equally wondrous? Is somewhere in the cycle of nature something now missing, because I have named this snowflake Ferdinand and declared him mine own?

This so deeply troubled The Snowflake Collector that he spent many hours sitting at his table in his very small kitchen, not eating anything, not even *Bündnerfleisch* and barely touching his *Chrüterschnapps,* wondering how, if ever, he could atone for this act of appropriation. Who am I, he thought, to claim such a beautiful thing? How dare I deprive it of its link to its past and its future? Is it not insufferably arrogant and presumptuous of me to make me his 'master'?

He felt the abyss of despair open up its gaping void before him, and the urge to throw his third, his successful case for the snowflakes into the fire overcame him, but he felt no power to let go of Ferdinand. Could it be, he wondered, in passionate silence, that I am already in love with him? Has making him mine already made me his just as much, am I already, only hours after capturing him, entirely under his spell? And this is only one, my first one, how will I bear adding to him? Will he and the power he has over me not become so overwhelming as to be meaningless? Will he and his fellows, his peers, entirely take over? Will I succumb to their unbearable potency?

The Snowflake Collector did not go to bed that night. Slumped over the table by the flickering flames in the stove, he sat there, clasping the glass plates between which he had immortalised – by, he felt, killing – his snowflake friend Ferdinand, and when he woke up in the morning, the blood from his thumb where the sharp edge of the glass had cut into his flesh had encrusted his hand and the table and also the glass, and a drop of his blood had seeped in between the two glass plates, and so together with his first snowflake there was now preserved there also a drop of himself, and he said to himself: so be it.

I shall surrender to the will of the universe, and if it is not the will of the universe it is the frivolity of my imagination I shall follow. Ferdinand will forgive me. Or maybe he can't. But I shall make his agony worthwhile: I shall share him with the world. And that way, maybe, he too, not just I, can have a purpose beyond our mere existence.

He put Ferdinand in his pocket and, still not having eaten anything, made his way down to the inn on the edge of the hamlet, an hour or so from his hut, and there introduced him – holding out his still unwashed, bloodied hand – to Yanosh. 'Look,' he said; and Yanosh took the plate from his hand and held it up against the light, and his eyes lit up with equal awe. Yanosh, after a minute or two of examining him took out his smartphone and photographed him with the light shining through him, and handed him back and asked: 'what name did you choose?'

'Ferdinand.'

'I like Ferdinand,' Yanosh said. 'I'll have to get hold of a macro lens for my camera, so I can take better pictures.'

7: Every Day Brought New Gifts Now

Every day brought new gifts now from the universe. There was Alison and Cassandra. Timothy, Lou and Lysander. There was tiny Frederick and the majestic Cassiopeia. It snowed for several days, and each day The Snowflake Collector got up with a spring in his step and, before doing anything else of significance, went outside with three glass plates prepared, no fewer, no more, and welcomed the snowflakes into his world. Lavinia. Esteban. Roswitha.

He had no system, no method; he had a passion and a beating heart, he had no words to describe these snowflakes he so collected, but he gave them names. Balthasar. Emilio. Blossom. Alexander. He realised that it was easier to let them settle onto dry cold glass plates and then fix them with just one drop of superglue, than it was to catch them into a drop of glue that was already there on the glass before it dried out. He learnt he had best cool down the glue too. Once or twice he made a mistake and instead of a single snowflake ended up catching a cluster, and sometimes he damaged a snowflake he had caught while applying a dab of glue to it, but with nothing else occupying his mind, and little else making demands on his time, he soon perfected his technique and sharpened his eye for the snowflakes that wanted to be part of his life now, accepted his invitation.

He learnt to be at ease now with his calling and considered it an invitation he extended to these snowflakes, a welcome, and not a trap. Not a prison. And before long the first of the sturdy wooden cases he had made began to fill up, and when Yanosh came to visit him now, and nodded his wordless 'hello', to be answered by The Snowflake Collector in kind, he found on the table in The Snowflake Collector's very small kitchen, and on the window sill and on the short shelf, these glass plates which had in them indescribable treasures: imprints of crystals, characters written by nature. And Yanosh brought along now not just his smartphone but also his camera for which he had bought a second-hand macro lens online with money he had been given by his mother Yolanda's employer, the inn's landlord, for a few hours' work every day in the kitchen, and he took these glass plates and photographed them, finding new, better ways of taking his pictures each time.

When Yanosh showed The Snowflake Collector the pictures he took of his snowflakes on the display of his camera, The Snowflake Collector felt a well of love surge through his heart: a love for Ramira, Zahir and Kamala, but also for Yanosh for capturing them in their utter perfection and for taking the time and for having the care and for witnessing what he was doing and for allowing him to share.

He had not, in years, maybe decades, felt a love such as this, for another human being, a friend, or for the world and that which was in it and for the soul that infused his existence. And he was grateful. More grateful, more gracious, more humble, for it. More whole, he sensed, than he had ever been. Yes, he was able to say to himself now, looking at the pixels in which a snowflake he had captured was recaptured and re-rendered with such exquisite clarity and detail as his eye alone could never have seen or let alone shown, I am thus become The Snowflake Collector: it is so.

No sooner had this thought formed in his mind, this sensation expanded into his body, this certainty grown in his presence, than he also was sure that what he was doing was wholly inadequate. He almost felt a rumble of anger thunder up through his chest, but since anger was so alien an emotion to him, so futile, so unnecessary, he allowed it to disperse into simple dissatisfaction: it will not suffice to do this, he said to himself and to his unending surprise and the even greater surprise of Yanosh too, he said it out loud: 'this will not suffice.'

'These snowflakes: they deserve better. These glass plates that I have cut for them and this case I have built: they are wrong. I cannot flatten these snowflakes! They are not created in two dimensions. I have to find a whole new solution.'

With this he went around his kitchen and he took each one of the glass plates he'd cut, into which he had already preserved all the snowflakes that made up his collection so far, and he looked at each one and apologised. Anna. Matthias. Rodrigo. Filomena. Lucas. One by one he held them up before his eyes and bade their forgiveness. 'You have all been wronged,' he told them, as he put them away in the case he had built for them with wood from a fir that had grown on his land by the stream, and he breathed a sigh of deep sorrow and said to Yanosh: 'I will have to start over again. I shall keep them, of course, they are now collected and to destroy them would be sacrilege, even though I have wronged them.' And he took all the glass plates he hadn't yet used and sat down at his kitchen table while Yanosh was watching in silence, and he started cutting them up, twice each again, and began to assemble them into cubes.

After an hour or so The Snowflake Collector had made maybe a dozen simple, clean-edged glass cubes, one inch by one inch by one, fixed and closed on five sides, with the sixth side left open. 'I will have to,' he said to Yanosh, 'find a liquid, a gel. Something that will preserve these snowflakes just as they are, that won't flatten them, won't deprive them of a dimension.' Yanosh nodded in quiet agreement and said, 'I'm going to look it up for you.'

8: It Was, in Every Imaginable Sense, a Disaster

No matter how Yanosh tried, no matter where he looked and what he put in his search field, the world did not seem to possess for The Snowflake Collector an answer. Innumerable were the sites and video clips that explained how to preserve snowflakes on microscopic slides or small sheets of acetate, using either – as he had been doing – superglue or hairspray or an artist's fixative; and they all arrived, going by the evidence Yanosh could find, at results similar to the ones that The Snowflake Collector so far had reached.

But this, Yanosh knew, for The Snowflake Collector had told him, would not suffice. He would need, The Snowflake Collector had said and determined, a way of collecting his snowflakes in the fullness of their dimensions. And while it may have been the case that in their majority these snowflakes seemed, at first glance, so flat as to fit neatly within a thin layer of superglue trapped between two small plates of glass, The Snowflake Collector knew that this was nothing but a deception. A deception and a crass simplification by the lazy mind.

In reality, all these snowflakes – even the flattest among them, but most certainly those that came in the shape of short studs or even, as often they did, in a formation of nearly flat hexagonal structures enjoined with, or indeed by, short column shaped ones – were miniature crystals of infinitesimal complexity. To squeeze them between two glass plates and store them flat in a wooden case, no matter how carefully crafted, was, to The Snowflake Collector, as looking at the world and declaring it a disk off the edge of which one might fall…

The Snowflake Collector knew, then, that he would have to develop his own substance. He would have to acquire some knowledge, and applying this knowledge he would, through a process of trial and error and elimination, have to come up with a liquid, a gel that would have just the right consistency, that would be clear as glass, and that would dry, at habitable temperatures, with untarnished translucence and would keep the shape and the intricacy and the character of the snowflake he would encase in it, in three dimensions, for the relative eternity he or any other human being could envisage; not an eternity, then, perhaps, but a lifespan of civilisations: the extent of a physically appreciative intelligent presence on this planet.

A deep crisis of confidence soon engulfed him, for Yanosh's extended research online remained fruitless. The Snowflake Collector now even undertook his rare and adventurous journey two or three times, by yellow bus and little red train and larger green or white train along the lakes into the biggest of any of the cities in his country, and to the enormous library of the university there, to study the properties of chemical solutions at different temperatures and their reaction to coming in contact with ice. But hours and days and nights and weeks and months of toil both in theory in the city and in practice at home in his valley did not yield up to him any liquid or gel or substance of any kind that would catch a snowflake and leave it intact and absolutely unharmed, suspended in a glass cube in three dimensions, one inch by one inch by one.

The Snowflake Collector sensed the end of the season draw near, and with it he felt this abyss of despair once more gaping before him, calling him to fall, drawing him close to surrender, willing him to give in. He did not feel, The Snowflake Collector, that if in this undertaking, as in so many others before, he failed, he would find the strength, the courage, the spirit to pursue it again the next winter. Or any other endeavour. He was now, he felt certain, exhausted, spent. He had given the universe his all, and the universe had, once more, rejected his offering. Yet again, crushed by defeat and destroyed by his own, maybe lofty, ambition, he had exerted himself, but he had not excelled. It was, in every imaginable sense, a disaster.

The snow melted. The stream, where he had a small plot of land on which he planted two young fir trees for each mature one he cut down, had already swollen with the water from the fast disappearing masses of white that had covered the meadows and the sharp inclines of the mountainside, and The Snowflake Collector was no more. He had ceased to exist, his purpose evaporated like the miserable puddle of water left on the window sill from the erstwhile snow, with the warm morning sun. The devastation was drawn into the furrows of his troubled forehead, and when Yanosh now came to sit with him outside his hut, their silence was one of sadness and loss.

The stale stench of failure now clung about him, The Snowflake Collector knew, and he felt despair not just for himself but also for Yanosh. This friend. This loyal lad, still growing up, still becoming a person. Had he not let him down terribly too. Had he not drawn him into his project and made him a part of it, and did the ruins of it now not lie scattered before his innocent eyes, his young heart cut and bleeding; for what? A delusion? A whim? A fantasy? For a false and forever frustrated illusion that there could be such a thing as meaning, as purpose, as friendship and love?

Tears ran down The Snowflake Collector's face and fell on the cold folded hands in his lap and he felt he was already dead. Yanosh could not bear to look at him. But he sat still by his side and bore with him his pain. And thus they remained, awaiting in silence the dread bounce of spring.

9: So as Not to Chase Away its Wonder

It was a miserable Easter that The Snowflake Collector encountered, and Whitsun was worse. Day after day the sun rose, but not he, not for hours. Most days, he barely made it onto the bench outside his hut, and since he had no appetite, he didn't eat, and as he didn't eat he grew gaunt, and the listlessness in his heart turned the skin that hung off his bones grey and painted his spirit all bleak.

There would have been butterflies to colour his mind; there would have been cute little crocuses. The meadows turned yellow with dandelions and green with fresh, rich grass and there were the multitude of insects with their implacable buzz and their hum; and the cows returned with their picture book bells that lent the valley its melodic chime in the distance.

The Snowflake Collector cared aught. He went not on his walks and he neglected his wood by the stream. He missed Yanosh, whose visits had become sparse, but he could not bring himself to wander down the path to the inn, an hour or so from his hut, to nod his silent 'hello' to him there and ask for an ale from his mother Yolanda. There was no point now to any of it, the pointlessness of it all was complete.

It was an unusually sullen day in June – after a month of May full of sunny disposition, bordering on the obnoxious – when The Snowflake Collector was sitting on his bench outside his hut and saw Yanosh climb up the path at a pace. He was in no hurry, Yanosh, since he, much as The Snowflake Collector, had eschewed the notion of 'hurry', or rather had never embraced it, but he was a good and energetic walker, and he was young, and so wherever he went, he went with a stride.

Yanosh sat down next to The Snowflake Collector on his bench, but today he didn't even nod a 'hello', nor did he say anything, he just sat there, apparently more than a little perturbed. The Snowflake Collector did not speak either, but he looked over at him, to find his friend staring ahead of himself, at the ground. Something, The Snowflake Collector surmised, must have happened, most likely something to upset him, perhaps something that his mother Yolanda had said, though more likely something a teacher at school had remarked or something his inadequate peers had done; but to ask, The Snowflake Collector felt, was to pry, and it was not in his nature to pry, nor was it in Yanosh's nature to expect him to.

Thus the young lad who wasn't quite as young as sometimes he seemed and the old man who was nowhere near as old as he felt sat there in silence for an hour or two, until something occurred that took them both by surprise. It started to snow. They were in the mountains, at the end of the valley, near the glacier now slowly receding, just above the tree line, so snow in June was not unheard of for Yanosh and The Snowflake Collector, but although this had been an ill favoured month, they weren't expecting it now.

When Yanosh and The Snowflake Collector now looked at each other, they both burst out laughing. They had no good reason, it was just that they cut surreal figures in a picturesque setting at the onset of summer when it had started to snow, and at this precise moment, for the first time, they realised this. The Snowflake Collector got up and with a few moves cleared the wooden table outside his hut, then he went into his kitchen and brought out a box that had in it the glass cubes he'd made. He brought out the bottles of liquids that he had bought and mixed and experimented with throughout the winter, and he stood at the table outside his hut, Yanosh watching him in fascination, and, noting down ratios and combinations with a heavy pencil directly onto the heavy table, he began developing new solutions, one emerging from the other, building on any progress he was making and discarding any failures without grief.

Three hours and forty-odd minutes went by in this manner before he needed a short break for comfort, and he disappeared momentarily, leaving on his table three cubes, each with a marginally different solution in it, and maybe he forgot or maybe his subconscious willed him to omit laying any kind of cover on them, but Yanosh sat and watched in an astonishment that unclenched his own heart how a gorgeous snowflake eased itself directly into the cube in the middle, and stayed.

Yanosh got up from his bench, slowly. Carefully he advanced on the miracle he was sole witness to and hesitantly, reluctantly lest he should undo it, lest a shake or a wobble or the hot breath from his nostrils should disturb it, he, holding on to the weighty wooden table, squatted down and watched, and watched. He didn't notice that The Snowflake Collector had since appeared behind him and in turn observed the scene, from just a little distance, also so as not to chase away its wonder. Then The Snowflake Collector became aware of another fat snowflake making its way just about straight into the same cube and he darted forward and caught that one with his hand, while with his other hand supporting himself on Yanosh to avoid knocking the table. Softly now he covered the cube with its purpose-cut lid and squatted down beside Yanosh to examine its beauty.

It was perfect. The liquid, in which the snowflake now floated was completely clear and the snowflake was still intact: minutes after immersing itself, it retained its shape, its intricate structure, its delicacy. It was miraculous. But could it last? The temperature outside on this day was just a few degrees above freezing. Would the snowflake, once brought inside, now melt and dissipate into its ether? The Snowflake Collector barely dared touch it but he fixed the lid to its cube now with a permanent seal of glue and left it standing there. Time would tell. Snowfall in June doesn't tend to last very long: soon the sun would appear and subject his experiment to the most unforgiving of tests.

Yanosh went home as he usually did around this time when he had come to visit during the day, and The Snowflake Collector went inside his hut to lie down. He was exhausted. And although he had no certainty yet and certainly no evidence that this latest effort of his would bear fruit, that it worked, that his snowflake would still be there in the morning, he already sensed the unbearable burden of sorrow ease off his chest. Each breath of air he took in filled him deeper with reconciliation, and for a moment he remembered that he hadn't named this snowflake! No matter, he thought, as his eyelids grew heavy and he slowly surrendered to sleep: it can wait. If the snowflake is still a snowflake next time I wake, it shall have a name.

10: George

The moment he woke up the next morning, The Snowflake Collector had only one thought: 'George.'

That was his name. It would have to be. There was no other possibility. If he were still to be there, if the gel into which he had settled had not crushed him, or dried him out, or obliterated him; if he were still to be a snowflake today, then there was a chance – maybe a slim chance only, but a chance – that he would still be a snowflake tomorrow, and if he were to be a snowflake tomorrow, still, there may be a chance that the method had worked, that this gel was the formula that he would need to – be able to, now – apply. But time only would tell. Certainly, if he were to find him still there, where he had left him, on the kitchen table, then that would be a good sign. But it would be no more than that. And surely his name would have to be George.

The Snowflake Collector got up from his narrow hard bed and wandered slowly into the kitchen: a short distance that felt to him this morning eternally long. He did not want to cast his eyes over the table in the dim light that filtered through the small window, but before he could avert them, George had caught them, was calling them over to him: look at me, I am here! The miracle was complete.

Not only was he still there, he seemed to radiate, shine. Now, some fourteen hours after he had come into contact with the peculiar liquid inside the glass cube that had caught him, enveloped him, slowed him and then suspended him just precisely in time before he was able to sink to the bottom or to dissolve, he seemed made of crystal indeed: it was quite extraordinary. The Snowflake Collector lifted the cube from the table and held it up against the pale light in which particles of dust engaged in their strangely courteous dance, and a swell of joy welled up in his heart as he saw: George is alive! He was as alive as any snowflake that wasn't engaged in its own dance still, through the sky toward earth, could possibly be; he was vivid and compelling; he had as much character as any inanimate thing The Snowflake Collector had ever seen, and he knew now, for certain, The Snowflake Collector, that this was not a thing without soul: this was George, the most exquisite snowflake ever formed in the world, perfectly captured, by him.

The gel, overnight, had solidified into a firm but not hard cast that was still absolutely transparent and that seemed to allow George to breathe. Of course, The Snowflake Collector knew, in reality George did not breathe, and the cube was hermetically sealed, but it was a minimal malleability that seemed to keep George animated, if, certainly, no longer free. The Snowflake Collector put George down on the kitchen table and stepped outside his hut and wiped the thin layer of snow from the table that stood out there, and he found, as he knew he would, noted down on it the last set of proportions he had used, and he now copied them onto a piece of wood that he picked up from the ground, and took them inside: this was the key, and it was unique.

Not in the way he had heard on occasion some people call something 'unique' when they meant it was simply 'special', or 'well made', or 'quite interesting'. This was a thing that was one of a kind: no-one else had found it before him and maybe nobody else ever would, or would want to, again, and it was far from certain that it would stand the test of time that now loomed before it, but for the time-being this was what he himself had achieved, and so far it was good; and if George were still to be there in October, or in November, or even December, whenever next the valley would be covered in snow, then he would apply this same formula to make the gel in which to preserve other snowflakes, and he would store them in a new sturdy case he would build to accommodate the new dimensions of these cubes, and if the following year, and the year after, all these snowflakes, and George, were still there, then he would be who he had decided to be, who he felt in his heart and knew in his mind he needed to be: he would become The Snowflake Collector, and Yanosh would be able to take pictures of these snowflakes with his macro lens that he had bought for his camera, and everything would be just so.

After this short burst of snow in the middle of June, the valley soon reverted to summer, and The Snowflake Collector put George on his own in the new case that he'd built, and occasionally he would take him out to look at him in awe. Yanosh spent some time away as sometimes he did this time of year, but when he came back to The Snowflake Collector's hut late in August, he found him in a hopeful mood, and in good spirits. George was still there and he hadn't lost any of his intricate beauty. The gel that had nearly hardened, but not quite, was still exactly as clear and still just a little flexible; it hadn't solidified any further and nor had it softened, it had simply stayed as it was, neither hard nor soft, neither wet nor dry, neither hot nor cold, but all of these all at once and none of these, all at the same time.

The Snowflake Collector was ecstatic – quietly, inwardly so, as was his wont – at having, it seemed, found a way to preserve his snowflakes in their full three dimensions; but of course he was also worried, and gravely concerned: what about their fourth dimension, he wondered, and fifth? Even as I name these snowflakes and know that they each have a soul, how can I do that soul justice? How can I trap a snowflake and pat myself on the back, when I but caught it and barely scraped the surface of any understanding of what a snowflake truly is?

Yanosh was unperturbed by all this. 'You'll get to know them,' he said, in his simple, laconic tone that was never agitated, and never bored, 'and as you get to know them, they will reveal to you their fourth dimension, and fifth, and even, if they have one, their sixth.' This rang true with The Snowflake Collector, and he held the arm of Yanosh – the first time possibly he had ever done so – and said, 'thank you, Yanosh. I hope you are right.'

But what if he weren't right, what if what Yanosh had said was well intentioned, but simply not true? There was no way of knowing, there was no way of anticipating, there was no way of solving this problem now. All The Snowflake Collector could do now, and for the remaining months of the year, until snow returned to the valley, whenever that should happen to be, was to look after George and prepare himself, for winter would come and with it would come the moment of truth and only then, come the moment of truth, could he really commence with his task that was quite immense.

11: He Was, Now More Than Ever, His Own Man

Winter did return to the valley, a little later each year now, it seemed, and with winter returned the snow and with the snow began in earnest The Snowflake Collector's work.

He applied his formula and mixed according to it his extraordinary liquid that had just the right qualities, the exact consistency and molecular structure to capture snowflakes as they sank into it, without melting them, without damaging, harming them, but able to, so far as the continued existence of George suggested, preserve them for not only seconds or minutes or hours or days, but for months, maybe years. And he quickly found that the differentials of success over failure were minuscule. It took him many days and every day several attempts just to recreate a small quantity of the solution, and even then the snowflake that sank into it only kept its shape for a moment before it melted and passed.

Not only were the proportions of the ingredients to each other of critical importance, but the stillness of the liquid inside the cube – one inch by one inch by one – and, particularly, the precise temperature at the point of entry made the difference between death and a continuation of life, in some sense, of the snowflake that was being captured. Even how long it took him to seal the cube after capturing a snowflake mattered to how likely the snowflake was to stay intact.

His task, he soon realised, was not just immense, it was also extraordinarily difficult and demanding. But he did not mind. And he no longer despaired. He had, on his shelf in his hut, one pristine, perfect specimen of a snowflake, the one he had named George, and George was still there, he still shone like a tiny beacon that whispered of the attainable, and as long as he was there, there was a point, there was a purpose, there was a reason, and if it was one reason only, to persist.

Innumerable may be the failures now – and innumerable, though they weren't, they felt – before The Snowflake Collector would succeed in capturing even just one snowflake as exquisite as George, but he knew now it was possible, and that was all he needed to know. And as he persevered he was able to, slowly, gradually, attain other, similar miniature triumphs. None, perhaps, felt as glorious as George had felt, that surprising day in the wrong season when he had landed upon him, but each brought its own little joy, its own advancement, sometimes followed, shortly after, by a setback, a failure, even a minor catastrophe. But none now were in that sense a disaster.

He carefully crafted more sturdy boxes for the glass cubes that he made, and he filled one, then another, with snowflakes that he named, each as he caught it; and regularly Yanosh would come up to his hut, and now they often found they had something to talk about. They still mainly just nodded at each other to signal 'hello', and then when they parted they signalled 'goodbye' in a similar way, but as The Snowflake Collector himself now spent so little time sitting outside his hut and so much time cutting glass plates, assembling them into cubes, building boxes, mixing liquids, studying the effects these liquids had on the snowflakes and the effects that these snowflakes had on the liquids, and perfecting his practice, Yanosh seldom now simply sat outside The Snowflake Collector's hut to watch him, or watch the world go by – which didn't go by here, as both of them knew, even though both of them knew also that it also never stood still – but helping him, if there was some way to help, or, if not, then photographing these snowflakes in their exceptional beauty.

And as The Snowflake Collector honed his technique, he became not only better at what he was doing, he slowly turned into an expert at snowflake collecting, and beyond an expert he became a master at it. He began to understand these snowflakes as they spoke to him in their silent presence, and he learnt to absorb and to internalise their essence. He still wasn't able to communicate it, but he felt that maybe that wasn't so necessary now, because as he was becoming a master at snowflake collecting, Yanosh kept taking pictures of them, and he too got better at taking pictures of snowflakes, and although he did not have any desire to become an expert at snowflake photography, or let alone, in these young years of his, a master at anything yet, his pictures were astonishingly compelling, and, as he did with any picture he had taken and of which he thought that someone might like it, he posted some of these snowflakes online, and predictably people were struck by their wondrousness.

Without knowing it, The Snowflake Collector acquired a following. Yanosh didn't make much of the fact that the picture collections he set up on his social network began to spread and attract the attention of admirers all over the world. To him, that was just what happened when you posted pretty pictures online. But there was something about these snowflakes that set them apart from other pictures of snowflakes. Maybe it was the way in which they were kept, in these glass cubes, floating, it seemed, in a gel that lent them their luminous sheen; maybe it was the names that The Snowflake Collector gave them and that Yanosh faithfully transferred when he labelled these pictures; or maybe it was just the unfussy tenderness of Yanosh's framing, the gentle exposure and understated postproduction that made them look as complex as nature and as simple as geometrical art: it was impossible to tell.

What was certain was that The Snowflake Collector's snowflake collection grew, and as it grew and grew more captivating, it captured the imagination of more people, and it wasn't so long before some of these people, either because they happened to be in the relative vicinity of the valley already, or because they felt this was as good a reason as they needed to come to the valley, started to visit him. The Snowflake Collector was not keen on visitors, by and large, but as they were few only in number, and their appearance in the valley was infrequent enough, he welcomed them and introduced them to some of his snowflakes, individually, selectively, and by name; and the visitors would tell their friends about these encounters in conversations and post their own pictures of the snowflakes and of The Snowflake Collector, recounting their stories; and invariably, as The Snowflake Collector's reputation spread, 'the media' finally cottoned on to him. At first it was just a young journalist who took an interest in these curious tales she'd heard and who was fascinated by the pictures she 'discovered' when doing a quick search online, and she came to the valley and did a sensitive portrait of him that appeared somewhere in a paper that few people read.

This was picked up by another and soon yet another, and without ever wishing it so, The Snowflake Collector found himself famous. He did not understand the reason for this. He was The Snowflake Collector, what he did was collect snowflakes. He was generous with his snowflakes and he would introduce them to anyone who came to him curious to meet them, but he did not think that what he was doing – although as a task immense and demanding – was something that anyone else so disposed as he could not do.

The people who came to visit him, most particularly those who came from 'the media', found this quaint and endearing. The Snowflake Collector knew they were patronising him, but he did not mind about that either. He felt no anger towards them, and no contempt. These were the same people – not the same individuals, of course, but broadly speaking representatives of the same culture – that had for decades ignored and belittled him. Even ridiculed him. But those long years he had spent in the big city among them, trying to be taken seriously by them, attempting to create, wishing himself noticed by them, they had washed away with the meltwater that had rushed down the stream by which he kept his small plot of land with the trees that he planted, two for each one that he cut down to use for his modest needs. He had no fear of them now and no regard other than the regard he had, and had kept, always, for all human beings: they were friends in as much as they were certainly not enemies, for to grant someone the status of enemy is to give them power over you, and The Snowflake Collector had long ceased to give anyone power over himself. He was, now more than ever, his own man.

12: There Was Nothing Now But the Snow

When Yanosh found him, lying in the snow, he was as cold as the earth and as grey as the sky and as still as the heart that stopped beating. For many years, Yanosh had been coming to visit him, up at the end of the valley, even though he had long ceased to live in the hamlet outside the village, an hour or so's walk from the hut; and for many days The Snowflake Collector had been lying on the ground in the snow, on his back, his eyes facing up to the sky whence the snowflakes kept on descending.

These eyes, these cheeks, now sunken-in, these bristles of his beard, had long been covered by a blanket of white, and no birds were up here, this time of year, to pluck at the eyeballs, no vermin or hungry beast to tear at his flesh: he was already at rest. When Yanosh wiped the snow off his face, he saw that he'd closed his eyes and fallen asleep, there was no stare, there was no anguish in his features, there was nothing now but the snow.

He had long since grown at one with the universe, The Snowflake Collector, and nothing else mattered now. He had his meaning. He had his hut and his priceless collection of snowflakes which grew every day that the sky brought him snowflakes, he had a friend in Yanosh who came to see him every so often when he was in the country and a friendly face in Yanosh's mother Yolanda whom he saw at the inn on the few and fewer occasions he went down there for an ale, and he had the occasional visitor who had seen Yanosh's pictures of his snowflakes online or read about his collection in an article or heard about it from a local or an acquaintance, or learnt of it from a book.

Very rarely, hardly ever, had he accepted an invitation to go down from the valley and undertake a journey, by bus and by train and sometimes by plane, to one of the cities to address a conference or a symposium or a convention and talk about his understanding of snowflakes.

He knew that he could not communicate his understanding of snowflakes to the world by talking about them, and he couldn't by writing about them – which he never attempted – and he couldn't by showing them to Yanosh who photographed them and posted his pictures of them online. But he felt he could perhaps give something back to a universe that had, in the end, and on balance, treated him fairly and with such care, by humouring these people who now, now that he no longer craved their attention, clamoured for him and professed that they longed to know of his mind.

He knew, The Snowflake Collector, that snowflakes had many dimensions – seven at least he could think of, but probably more – and he could see these dimensions clearly and distinctly in his mind's eye even though he knew he would never be able to see them with his physical eye, nor represent them visually, nor show them to Yanosh, or anyone else. He would not be able to explain them, nor would he ever be able to convince anyone in the world that these snowflakes had many dimensions, seven at least, but probably more, because he knew enough of the world and its violent rejection of anything it couldn't see with its eyes and measure with its instruments and comprehend in the context of its current science to realise that any attempt of his to do so would remain futile; he knew of the world's irrational fear of anyone and anything it deemed irrational, and he felt not foolish enough, any more, to argue or make a case.

What he could do, and did do, was to collect these snowflakes in their physical three dimensions as one who knows of their further dimensions and as one who knows that what he was able to show Yanosh, and what Yanosh was able to show the world, was not just less than half of what a snowflake was, but only the tiniest fraction, because he also knew, The Snowflake Collector, that each additional dimension does not add to a thing as much as the previous one, but each additional dimension increases the complexity of the thing exponentially.

He would never, he knew, be able to explain this or convince anyone that this was so, but the thought of it alone made The Snowflake Collector extraordinarily happy; and elated by this happiness, he felt, for the rest of his days on this earth, in his valley, in love. He was in love with George, the first snowflake he had successfully collected by his own particular method, and he was in love with Yanosh whose loyal friendship sustained him, and he was in love with the valley and the mountains that made the valley, and with the stream that ran through it, and with the trees that he planted on the plot of land that he kept by the stream, two young trees for each old tree he cut down, and with the old trees he cut down just as much, and he was in love with Yolanda who served him his dependable ale when he went to the inn on few and fewer occasions, and he was in love with the universe and he sensed, because of this, the universe, in equal measure, love him.

And he knew, then, The Snowflake Collector, that he would be able to communicate to the world his understanding of snowflakes and their dimensions not through words, not through the snowflakes he collected in the glass cubes that he cut, one inch by one inch by one, not through the pictures that Yanosh took of these snowflakes in their glass cubes, floating in the mysterious, but not magical, gel that he had developed, not through drawing, describing or dancing them, but through love.

And if only one other person – be it Yanosh, or be it Yolanda, or be it a random visitor to his hut, or be it someone who came across him or his snowflakes or his story somewhere – were to experience that love and through that love these dimensions and through these dimensions were to know of the soul of the snowflake, then his work, he was certain, was worthwhile and his communion complete.

He was now, he felt, as he took all the glass cubes from the cases he had carefully crafted, which, over the years, had needed their own formidable shed, and broke each one open and allowed the gel to evaporate and the snowflake he had collected in it to escape back into the universe and become what it needed to become next, and, having spent many hours so freeing his snowflakes, lying down on his back in the snow, welcoming down upon him new snowflakes that he no longer now would collect but simply become a part of, he was now, he knew, as he lay there, after another hour or so closing his eyes and holding his hands open to the sky and allowing the blood to drain from his brain and the pulse to ebb from his temples, he was, now that he had been and no longer needed to be The Snowflake Collector, he was now at one with it all.

Lightning Source UK Ltd.
Milton Keynes UK
UKOW07n1601280317
297717UK00001B/1/P

9 781684 181803